THE GOOD GOBLIN

by

DAVID MCELROY

ISBN-13: 978-1974364077
ISBN-10: 1974364070

Cover design: Ashleigh McElroy

First Edition

To my grandma, it took ten years but I finally did it. Thanks for always listening and encouraging me.

To my wife, Ashleigh, for your unending support and artistic talents.

CONTENTS

NOVEMBER 1900 — DECEMBER 1901

1.

NOT ALL GOBLINS ARE BAD

Not all goblins are bad. To be sure, the vast majority of them are and before I told you otherwise, there's no doubt that you considered the idea that goblins are bad an existential truth. Something so blatantly obvious and factual as the sky is blue, ice is cold, and water is wet.

However, many centuries ago, there was a goblin who lived beneath a small hillock in the English countryside. This goblin was in the habit of feeling sympathy for passing travelers who were exhausted from the journey, for the goblin's hillock was many miles from the nearest village or waterway.

The goblin, being a goblin, was also quite adept at magic, especially potion-making. He had concocted a brew many years prior that, when drunk out of his enchanted drinking horn, would revive the drinker instantaneously and give her or him the strength to go on for weeks without the need for other sustenance.

So it was that whenever one of these weary travelers happened upon his hillock and cried out in bitter exhaustion, the goblin would fill his drinking horn, approach the traveler, and offer his special potion to them.

Years went by and, before long, the existence of the goblin and the magic potion went from a whisper to rumor to accepted fact, and soon travelers began to make pilgrimages toward his hillock in the hopes of meeting with the strange hermit and tasting his enchanted drink.

All was well and the goblin was more than happy to help any passersby for they all showed him great appreciation and kindness. Until one day, when a boastful, proud, greedy knight made his way to the hillock. He had been searching several months for the goblin and was overjoyed to find him at last. The goblin emerged from his hermitage and presented the enchanted drinking horn to the knight. The knight took the horn, drank from it, and without a word of thanks, turned back the way he had come, the drinking horn still in hand.

Proud of his odious deed, the knight boasted to anyone and everyone that he happened upon about his capture of the relic. However, this did not have the effect that he had hoped for. Within a month, a great king had caught wind of the actions of the knight and promptly had him thrown in a dungeon for the rest of his days.

Unfortunately, the drinking horn was not returned to its rightful owner and the goblin never again showed himself to a human. Thus, the story of the benevolent goblin with the enchanted potion passed into legend and folklore.

＊ ＊ ＊

This story is not about that goblin but the repercussions of the greedy knight's actions against him are present all throughout our protagonist's life and without that single treacherous act, his story would have played out quite differently.

His name was Ben and to a human's eye, he was no different than any other goblin: short of stature, long ears that ended in sharp points, and skin that was green like the needles of a pine. He had a short crop of dark hair on his head, for long hair was reserved only for goblins who were the most honored among their race — something Ben was not – and eyes that were the deep, peaceful green of the sea at dusk.

What truly set him apart was something that only a goblin would notice. Unbeknownst to humans, goblins possess an extra sense called *kenna*. With *kenna*, they can feel each other's presence, tell the sort of mood another might be in, and when there's something in your soul, the very core of your being, that's not like everyone else, they can feel that, too.

From the moment Ben was born, they could feel his difference. No one knew exactly what that difference was for sure until he reached five years of life, the age when goblins begin their lessons.

It was discovered that he showed very little connection to his sense of *kenna*, had a much more mild and gentle demeanor, and above all else, unlike every other goblin, he alone did not seem to possess an inherent loathing for all humankind.

So, as is unfortunately common among all living beings who possess even the slightest difference from others, Ben was shunned. Even being the son of the goblin leader, the Great Hob of Jotunfell, gave him no advantages. In fact, if anything, it only made them despise him more. For how could someone with such a rich and true bloodline have the impudence to be born different?

Ben's only comfort was in his books. The art of storytelling was greatly revered among goblinkind and in this, Ben shared a slight similarity. However, he had no interest in the great goblin epics, the sagas of goblin heroes long since passed, or the subtle poetry describing the beauty that could be found in the destruction of man. Ben's interest lay solely in the stories written by humans. He loved the dramas of the downcast as told by Dickens, the strange science fiction of Wells, the clever genius of Doyle, and even the bard himself.

The great majority of his time was spent reading in isolation, and when he wasn't reading, he was on the hunt for new books. As luck would have it, the traveling merchant, who always seemed to have a human book or two on hand, cared not about the sense of his being but only for the color of his money. What little money Ben had was earned by pawning small trinkets and decorations from his room and then spent purchasing books.

It was through these books that he came to learn of the vast world beyond the high walls of Jotunfell, a city he had never been permitted to leave. Upon reaching the age of nineteen, the temptation for that world consumed him and Ben finally decided to sneak away, filled with the hope that perhaps, like the merchants, not everyone would judge him for who he could not help to be.

2.

AMONG HUMANS

Ben's escape from his homeland was perhaps a little less grand an adventure than the one he might have imagined. He had perceived himself in the role of the Man in the Iron Mask, fighting his way to freedom from his oppressors. However, he realized that without musketeers to help him, this scenario was highly unlikely. As it turned out, Ben's escape was much more akin to that of another Dumas hero, Edmond Dantes from *The Count of Monte Cristo* — though without the dead body.

While buying books one crisp, late autumn morning, Ben fully realized what it meant to be a *traveling* merchant: one could come and go from the city whenever one pleased. When Ben was sure that he was the book peddler's only customer, he approached him and explained his idea. The peddler was a frost goblin, who in contrast to their namesake had slightly less icy demeanors than their grassland cousins, and had developed a fondness for Ben. He had personally witnessed the cold treatment with which the young goblin was shown by his brethren and so, to Ben's surprise, he agreed.

That afternoon, as the peddler was packing up for the day, Ben snuck into his wagon, covered himself with canvas sacks, and made his escape from Jotunfell. The peddler took him as far as Saint Louis, the closest human settlement, which was about a day's ride to the north and east. Ben briefly fantasized about staying with the peddler, but he knew that if his father ever discovered the truth of how he had escaped, the peddler would be punished severely for abducting the son of the Hob, and Ben couldn't risk his savior coming to any harm on his account.

On the night he arrived in the city, the first snowfall of the year drifted down from the sky. As he stood across the river from the city, he was overwhelmed. Both by the beauty of the human settlement, standing tall and proud on the banks of the mighty Mississippi River, and by the sense of relief that he felt. In that moment, he truly breathed easy for the first time. The weight and burden that had gripped him his entire life seemed to lift, leaving him lighter and freer. Perhaps, he thought, in this place, he might find another like him. Not a goblin, of course, but a kindred spirit. From what he knew of the tense relations between humans and goblins, he realized it wouldn't be easy or perhaps even likely. But there was a chance, no matter how slight, and that was more than he had ever had.

It didn't take him long to realize just how right he was. While on an emotional and philosophical level he was very akin to the humans who were now his neighbors, he was still a goblin in form, and they had no interest in looking past their differences to their similarities.

You would be hard-pressed at that time in history in that part of the world to find a single human whose life had not been altered in some way by a goblin. Saint Louis was right on the edge of the goblin territories and the goblins were none too pleased to share such proximity with the hated and encroaching human race. So, whether it was a goblin stealing the humans' livestock, setting fire to their fields, or even killing a friend or relation, humans had every reason to be wary when a goblin crossed their path.

It took him over six weeks to find any employment. At that point, he had not eaten for days and if goblins required as much food as humans, he might have starved to death before his story had truly begun. He had spent his first few days going from shop to shop, seeking employ while his clothes were still clean and he was mildly presentable. He had barely gotten his request off his lips, though, before he was dismissed with scoffs, slanders, and, at times, shouts of anger.

After much persistence, lowering of his prospects, and a short spell where he was forced to beg on the street, an experience that humbled him even further than he would have thought possible, he at last obtained employment.

Unfortunately, no job managed to last more than a week. Even if his employer was willing to give him the work, his fellow workers were always unwilling to work alongside a goblin.

He jumped from job to job. Among other things, he worked as a street sweeper, a dock laborer, a muckraker, a chimney sweep, and, for an hour only, a fishmonger.

The months went by and before long, despair began to set in. He was on the brink of either going back to Jotunfell in defeat or possibly seeking out the frost goblins when he was offered a job with the city's Lamplighter's Guild. The guild was responsible for lighting the street lamps every night, but in addition, they acted as a night watch, informing the proper authorities if they found anything amiss. It was the latter of these two tasks to which Ben was assigned.

His post was the lighthouse in the middle of the Mississippi River on the outskirts of Saint Louis. The lighthouse was the first place where trouble from the north and east could be spotted before it arrived in the city and the guild member who had offered him the post knew well the keen sight of a goblin and judged him ideal for such a job. In addition, he also received room and board in the very lighthouse where he worked.

Even though the job itself was a lonely one, sitting in a lighthouse all night and sleeping all day, Ben was happy to have a warm bed, clean clothes, and enough food to sustain him once again.

3.

A GOBLIN ON WATCH

"Something's not right."

It was Ben's sixth night on the job and up until that moment, it had been quiet and uneventful. He had quickly taken to his new home, even though it was much less grand than the Great Hob's Keep. The lighthouse was constructed primarily of stone blocks with a green roof the shade of oxidized copper. It stood at least fifty feet tall, a true sentinel of light on the river during dark, moonless nights.

There were six flights of stairs with a set of

rooms at the juncture of each. Ben's room was on the fifth floor, where the conical structure was almost at its smallest diameter. The room was small, barely large enough for a bed, a small table, and a single gas lamp, but it was his and he cherished it. What books he had managed to bring, he stashed under the bed and spent his short amounts of free time reading and re-reading them.

The first five nights of his watch consisted of sitting on his perch atop the lighthouse, staring into the darkness, and seeing nothing staring back for ten straight hours a night. Now, however, he was watching something that was all wrong.

He was looking toward the docks, which stretched out along the city's riverside border for nearly a mile. It was an area he was somewhat familiar with, having performed several of his previous jobs there. During the day, ships bustled in and out of the port, large men hauled great crates of goods on their backs to the warehouses, and the smoke from the stacks gave the whole place a sepia hue. At night, though, it was quiet, save for the birds and the chiming of the nearby clock tower.

In the early morning's light, he could make out two people walking. The first was a young woman, whom he recognized as a fellow member of the Lamplighter's Guild. She had relieved him of his watch two mornings prior and Ben had been so struck by her gentle beauty that he had failed to utter a single word.

The second person he immediately recognized as well. The man who walked not twenty paces behind the young woman was a pickpocket named Sawyer, a man whom Ben had been unfortunate enough to run into during his time working on the docks. In fact, the pickpocket had stolen Ben's only earnings mere moments after he had been relieved of his employment. Everyone who worked or hung around the docks knew Sawyer, and if he was as close as twenty paces behind you, trouble would soon follow.

Ben waited a few moments longer, hoping that the thief would either change direction or the young woman would make it to the small rowboat used to reach the lighthouse before Sawyer reached her. However, when it became clear that neither were likely to happen, Ben did the only thing he could think to do. He cleared his throat, cupped his hands to his mouth, and shouted at the top of his lungs.

"Look out behind you! Look out behind you!"

Ben's shout was strong and true. Unfortunately, there were at least three hundred yards of river between the lighthouse and the dock. For that reason, and because the wind was unusually strong that morning, the goblin's words were lost on the breeze. He tried again but quickly realized his attempts were futile.

Frantically, he looked around him at the area where he had been perched every night that week. In addition to the large gas-lit torch at its center, there was a walkway that circled the torch, two crates for watchers to sit on, and leaning in the shadow of one of those crates, a loaded rifle. At least, Ben hoped that it was loaded.

He glanced back at the dock. Sawyer had halved the distance and the young woman was still completely unaware of his soft-footed presence. Ben hurled himself at the rifle, pulled the lock to full cock, and fired straight down into the river. The jolt of the recoil sent the small goblin reeling and his slammed against the glass wall that encased the torch.

His shoulder roared with pain, worse than he would have imagined possible, but he forced himself to his feet and peered back to the dock. Sawyer had disappeared and the young woman, who must have sprinted to the rowboat, was now sitting in the vessel and staring at the lighthouse with wide, searching eyes. Ben was about to wave to her when a strong hand grasped his aching shoulder and he crumpled under the pressure.

"What is the meaning of this?" shouted a clearly enraged voice.

Ben looked up at the man holding him. He was most likely a young man, but the wrinkles on his brow, the darkness of his sun-soaked skin, and the weariness in his eyes made him look much older.

"Do you not speak, *goblin*?" Ben couldn't help noticing that he practically spat the final word out, so distasteful was it to his tongue.

"Y . . . yes . . . yes, of course," the goblin stammered. He fought hard to regain some form of composure amid his fright and the piercing pain in his shoulder.

"Well then, *goblin*, do explain why you've

fired a rifle at apparently no one without authorization from your superior?"

It had never occurred to Ben that he would need permission to fire the rifle, but he didn't think saying so would grant him much leniency with this one.

"Across the way, at the docks, I saw . . . I saw a woman . . ."

"And you thought you'd display your brutish bravado by firing a large weapon into the air?"

Ben shook his head. The mere thought of him even possessing anything close to bravado, brutish or otherwise, was enough to make him laugh under ordinary circumstances.

"Of course not. She was being followed by a thief called Sawyer. I was merely warning her."

The man's eyebrows raised slightly at the name Sawyer. This was good, Ben thought, that he knew the name. Perhaps it might convince him of the explanation.

"So, you warned her by firing a weapon at

her?"

Ben couldn't help noticing that he was being spoken to as though he were a simpleton. He might have suspected it had to do with their differing ranks in the guild if it weren't for the man's constant use of the word 'goblin.'

"I fired into the river," he responded, reliving the jolt of the recoil as he said it.

The man stared at Ben a moment longer and then shook his head. "That's still no excuse for using an unauthorized . . ."

"She's a member of the guild," Ben interjected, fearing that he might not get another chance to speak.

This had the effect Ben had desired. The man stopped short and, for the first time, peered over the edge of the lighthouse wall toward the docks. He stared and seemed to be considering his options carefully. After several tense minutes of silence, he turned his attention back to Ben.

"Very well, I shall report this to the guild master and see what he thinks. Do you know the name of the woman?"

"No . . . no, I don't. I just recognized her because she relieved me a few nights ago."

The man nodded. "Come with me," he said in a low monotone.

The man descended the stairs and Ben followed. He led him into a door on the third floor of the lighthouse. It was a door that was usually closed, and Ben had assumed the room belonged to someone important. The man opened the door and strode into the room, taking a seat behind the large desk at the opposite side.

Like every room in the lighthouse, it was small, but this room, unlike the others, was well-furnished with fine wooden furniture and soft, padded chairs. There was even a large rug on the floor to soften the cold, hard, wood planks. There was a window behind where the man sat and the dawning sun was shining brightly through it. Ben squinted as he entered the room and sat in one of the two chairs on the other side of the desk.

For several, long, tense minutes, not a word was spoken. The man rifled through papers in the desk's drawers, pulling out many different official-looking forms. When he had found all the pages he needed, he slowly began to write on them with a black pen and even blacker ink. When he finally paused in his writing, he looked up at Ben.

"What is your name, *goblin*?"

Ben flinched at the last word again. He had seen much discrimination against his race while in Saint Louis, but he had never felt the scorn and biting condemnation as much as from this man. He wondered what could have happened for him to feel this way.

"Ben . . . Tamorensson."

The man's eyebrows shot up and his eyes

grew wide.

"Tamorensson? As in the son of Tamoren, the Hob of Jotunfell?"

Ben nodded.

"I see, and so, just to clarify your supposed story, you saw a girl you recognized as a member of the guild being stalked by a thief. You warned her by firing a rifle shot into the river. Is that about right?"

"I tried shouting first," he said dumbly.

"You tried shouting first," the man repeated slowly, mockingly. He stared at Ben a moment longer and then wrote it down on the page. Several more minutes of listening to the pen scratch its way across the paper ensued. Then the man sighed, gathered up his pages, and tidied them into a neat stack.

"Very well, I'll be turning this in to the guild master. It will be up to him to decide your future with the guild. I, however, don't believe a word of your story. It's ludicrous at best, and there is no evidence. It's much more likely that you're an undercover agent and you were trying to assassinate a target using your newfound position in our society."

Ben shook his head fiercely and could feel his eyes growing hot. The absolute injustice of what this man was saying stung him to his very core.

"That's not true, I'm telling the truth!"

The man scoffed. "Unfortunately, as you'll find, a goblin's word doesn't mean much in the human world. I doubt you'll find anyone who would believe your story."

"Actually . . ."

Both the man and Ben jumped at the sound of a new voice entering the room. It carried a great strength in its depth, and at the same time it was clearly warm and welcoming.

Ben turned to see the owner of the voice walking toward him, supported by a gnarled cane. He was a large man and very stocky, with a long beard of brown and gray whiskers and hair to match. He was exactly as Ben had imagined the Vikings to look like in the Norse Eddas that he loved to read.

The bearded man sat down next to him just as the other man behind the desk stood up.

"Guild Master, please, by all means, take my seat."

The bearded man smiled and waved a hand.

"It's alright, Jacob, I'm quite comfortable here." He turned to Ben and smiled. "And after walking up all of those damned stairs, I don't think I could get myself back up again so soon anyway."

Ben felt himself smiling back, he couldn't help it. He had been hired with the guild master's blessing but had never actually met him. The man behind the desk, Jacob, sat back down nervously.

"You were saying, Guild Master," he said when he had re-situated himself.

The guild master smiled and drew his kind gaze from Ben to Jacob.

"Ah, yes. I was saying that, actually, I do happen to believe his story."

Jacob looked aghast.

"But, but, he's a goblin. Do you know who his father is?"

The guild master, continuing to smile, nodded his head. "I do."

"And you still trust him, knowing full well that he is the son of the Hob of the largest goblin settlement in the Americas?"

"I do."

Jacob shook his head in absolute disbelief. "But there's no proof!" he shouted.

The sudden shout caused Ben to jump slightly in his seat, but the guild master remained unmoving.

"Actually," the guild master said again, "there is. It seems that the young lady to whom our goblin friend here was trying to warn, corroborated much of his story. She is downstairs if you'd like to speak with her yourself. Apparently, she didn't see exactly who was following her but after she heard the warning shot, she did turn and see a man fleeing."

Jacob obviously couldn't believe the turn this situation had taken. "But the rifle, he had no right to fire it," he said sternly, in what was clearly a final, fleeting effort on his part.

"That is true, however, it is there for emergency purposes. There are several other options that he could have taken before resorting to the rifle. However, as he is new to the job and obviously had to think quickly, I believe some leniency is in order and I do not fault him for his decision."

The guild master turned back to Ben, his smile wider than ever.

"At the end of the day, you aided a fellow guild member and no one was hurt in the process. I personally think you are to be thanked, so, thank you."

If Jacob was surprised at this turn of events, it was nothing compared to Ben. He had never been spoken to so warmly before by anyone: human or goblin. He sat there in stunned silence, at a loss for words. The best response he could produce was a nod of his head.

The guild master didn't seem to notice, or perhaps didn't mind, the awkward reply. He patted Ben on the shoulder and then put all his weight onto his cane and pulled himself to his feet.

"I'll go ahead and take those with me," he said to Jacob, indicating the stack of pages.

Jacob looked down at the papers in a daze and then, remembering himself, grudgingly lifted the stack and handed it to the guild master, who nodded courteously and turned to exit the room. When he was gone, Jacob stood as well.

"You can go now," he said coldly to Ben. Without waiting for an answer, Jacob swept from the room.

4.

MARIBEL

Three more nights passed uneventfully and Ben had all but put the incident out of his mind. The only time it occurred to him was on the occasions when he passed by Jacob, who did everything possible not to notice the goblin's presence.

On the fourth night, however, Ben received a surprise visit.

It was near to dawn and his eyelids were heavy as his shift neared to a close. He was fighting hard to keep sleep from overcoming him when a voice sounded behind him, jolting him awake. Ben swung around and nearly fell out of his chair. At the top of the stairs stood a young woman, *the* young woman, the guild member he had aided.

She was exactly as he had remembered her: of average height for a human but at least a foot and a half taller than he was. She had long auburn hair, large blue eyes, and freckles on her cheeks.

He mentally counted the days and, sure enough, it was the same night that she had relieved him the week prior. Thinking this visit was nothing more than a simple shift change, Ben stood, stretched his near to numb legs, and walked toward the stairs, head down as he was accustomed to.

The woman, however, didn't move and the stairway wasn't wide enough for both to fit. He stopped short just before the moment he would have run into her. When he looked up, he saw that she was smiling at him and not just a casual, friendly smile but a truly warm smile that rendered him immobile.

"You're Ben, right?" she said gently. Her voice was soft but not meek. There was a strength to it that he instantly recognized.

He nodded awkwardly and wasn't sure if proper conversation etiquette required him to say something back. Apparently not, for she continued.

"I heard about what you did the other day and I wanted to thank you."

Ben felt his face begin to blush, which on a goblin's green skin took on an orange hue. Now he was completely stumped. This was only the second time he had ever been thanked. He had gotten away with an awkward nod with the guild master but felt as though he needed to say something this time, but what was he supposed to say? Was he supposed to say "thank you" in return? He knew there were words for this occasion but couldn't remember what they were. His mind retreated to its place of comfort, lost in the thousands upon thousands of words that it had consumed over the course of his life. Surely, there had been at least one occurrence of someone thanking someone in all those words. Then, suddenly, a line from *Twelfth Night* sprang to mind.

'I can no other answer make but thanks, And thanks; and ever thanks'

And the next line of response was . . .

"Tomorrow, sir, best first go see your lodging."

"What?" asked the young woman. Ben was mortified to realize that he had spoken that line aloud. Her confusion clearly showed it was not the correct response.

"Nothing," he stammered, his face turning more orange still.

The young woman considered the goblin for a few speechless moments. Ben kept his eyes down because he didn't know what else to do. Finally, she smiled again and put out a hand.

"My name is Maribel."

Without waiting for him to act, she leaned down, took his hand in hers, and clasped them together in a warm, friendly greeting.

"I'm Ben," he said, grateful for her intervention. He might have stood there for hours, uncertain what to do, if she hadn't quite literally forced his hand.

"I know," she said, smiling wider still. "I'm pleased to meet you."

Maribel released him and then took the seat he'd recently vacated. They spoke no more that morning but it was a conversation, if one could even term it as such, that Ben would remember for the rest of his days.

The next week, Maribel arrived a little earlier than before to take his place, so they had more time to talk. Their conversation was naturally awkward at first, but as Maribel seemed to be quite practiced in the art of socializing, it soon became more comfortable.

The same routine followed the next week and the week after. Each time, she arrived earlier than the last. Before long, they no longer only met once a week. And without realizing it, Ben had made his first friend.

5.

THE MAGICIAN'S ASSISTANT

Ben had lived in Saint Louis for almost eight months and yet he had never ventured beyond the docks and slums and into the city proper. His confinement was, of course, self-imposed. In the lower, seedier portions of the city, people mostly kept to themselves and with the constant river traffic and comings and goings of merchants, it wasn't altogether unheard of to see a goblin now and then. However, beyond the invisible line that divided the lower city with the upper and middle-classes, seeing a goblin was nigh unheard of. During his brief stint as a chimney sweep, he had spent several hours a day, gazing longingly at the great buildings in the heart of the city, knowing that it was a place where he would most likely never be welcome.

One day, however, an opportunity presented itself. He and Maribel had spent the last several hours of his shift talking, as had now become the custom. As he was getting ready to go get some sleep, she froze him in place with a question.

"Would you like to go lamp lighting with me tomorrow night?"

That question may not seem so shocking to most. However, it was so surprising to Ben that he was sure he hadn't heard her right.

"Excuse me?"

"I asked if you wanted to go lamp lighting with me on my route tomorrow night. That's my job the other six nights of the week. You could get out of the lighthouse for a while and see some more of the city."

Ben frowned. "And you really want me to go with you?"

Maribel shrugged nonchalantly. "Yeah, what's so surprising about that?"

Ben couldn't help laughing. "I'm a goblin. Nobody likes a goblin or wants to be seen with one."

"You really think I'm just like everybody else?" she asked, a slight note of irritation in her tone.

Ben shook his head. "Of course not, but . . . It's just that . . ."

Maribel stood up and put her hand on his shoulder. "Ben, we're friends, and if you haven't already noticed, I really don't care much what other people think."

He nodded and smiled.

"So, you coming then?" she asked.

"Of course," he said, even though the

prospect terrified him as much as it thrilled him.

❊ ❊ ❊

And so, as he crossed the invisible line that separated the part of the city he knew from the unknown with Maribel at his side, a tremendous sense of excitement and dread again filled him simultaneously. He fully expected to be chased and driven back to the docks, but he had made up his mind to attempt to enjoy the time he was given.

It was close to dusk and the horizon glowed orange while, up above, the encroaching night sky shone a brilliant purple. The autumnal equinox was three weeks past and the air was beginning to cool as the days grew shorter. Ben took a deep breath of crisp fall air and the first thing he noticed was the smell. The air was so much cleaner here. The repugnant odors of fish, grime, rotted food, and smoke were replaced by the delicious aromas of freshly baked bread, spices, lady's perfume, men's cologne, and fresh flowers.

It was a different world over here. The sound of a trumpet playing a smooth jazz beat filled the air. In fact, music seemed to be everywhere on this side of the city. Bells rang on the passing trolleys, wind chimes tinkled in open windows, and birds, who largely steered clear of the docks, save for the nasty gulls, twilled their sweet songs.

Maribel carried her lamplighter's pole resting against her shoulder, and Ben was about to ask a question about how exactly it worked when they noticed a large crowd of people gathered on a street corner up ahead. Maribel looked down at him and smiled.

"Now this is something you need to see!"

She grabbed Ben's arm and pulled him into the crowd. They jostled their way through until they got to a spot where they could see what everyone was looking at.

At the center of the throng of people was a

lone man speaking in a boisterous voice. His clothes were a veritable rainbow of colors with a purple jacket, bright red pants, yellow shirt, and to top it off, an aquamarine top hat. He wore gloves that were so white, it looked as though he had never touched a thing whilst he had them on.

"Friends, friends, please gather round!" he shouted to the crowd. "I am the Great Percival the Perplexing!"

The crowd applauded enthusiastically and the man took a bow.

"May I pose you all a question? What makes plants grow?"

He stopped and looked around at all the faces that were staring at him in rapt attention.

"You there," he approached a girl of about eleven years of age who was standing next to a man that Ben assumed was her father. "What makes plants grow?"

She looked terrified at being singled out by

the magician but said in a hardly audible voice, "Water?"

Percival smiled.

"Indeed, yes, my dear!" He walked around and stopped at a middle-aged man in a smart suit. "What else, sir?"

"Well, sunlight."

"Quite right, quite right." He moved to an elderly woman next. "What else?"

"Fresh soil and fertilizer."

"Excellent! Four out of five!" He approached a young woman, whose hand he took and kissed with a short bow.

"And what else does a plant need to grow?" he asked.

The woman opened her mouth to speak but froze. At last, she blushed and shook her head.

"Anyone? Can anyone assist this lovely young lady? Who knows what else is needed?"

The crowd murmured softly amongst themselves but no one answered. Finally, Ben blurted out, "time!"

All eyes turned to Ben and the crowd shifted away from the goblin whom they had just noticed was there. Percival the Perplexing was not deterred, though. He walked straight to Ben, nodding his head all the while.

"Excellent, young sir! That is indeed correct! Would you mind assisting me with a simple demonstration?"

The last thing Ben really wanted was to stand in front of a crowd so obviously shaken at his presence, but Maribel gave him a little shove and Percival wrapped an arm around him and led him to the center of the circle.

"Just stand here, and I'll let you know when I need you," he whispered to Ben.

Then he turned back to the crowd.

"Exactly as you have said: water, sunlight, soil, fertilizer, and time. The first four are easy enough, but time is a fickle friend. A hungry man may have a seed and enough water, sunlight, soil, and fertilizer to sustain it. But when you add the element of time, he will die of starvation long before the seed bears fruit. What if, though, you could remove time as a barrier?"

He reached into his jacket and produced a large plum seed. He held it up for the crowd to observe and then he leaned down. On the ground was a pot filled with soil and a pitcher of water. He placed the seed into the pot and poured water over it. Then he set the pot down at Ben's feet and handed him a large green cloth.

"Good sir, if you would be so kind, please hold this cloth over the pot so that it is not visible. We must isolate time so that it may speed up from where it remains ever-flowing at a constant speed."

Ben did as he was instructed and Percival pulled out a flute from another of his inner jacket pockets. He waved the flute around the covered pot three times and each time, he chanted, "Grow, grow, grow!"

With each passing of the flute, Ben felt a shift under the cloth, until after the third pass, his arms were forced upward. Percival replaced the flute in his jacket and with a flourish pulled the cloth from the pot, revealing a plum tree that was taller than Ben, complete with enough plums on its branches for everyone in the audience.

The crowd cheered enthusiastically. Once Percival had handed out all the plums, the crowd dispersed. The young girl, the one who had earlier suggested water, broke away from the group and began to help the magician pack his things into a large sack. When this was finished, he approached Ben, who was still in awe, and held out his hand.

"Thanks for the help, kid," he said.

"You're welcome," Ben replied, shaking the proffered hand.

"This is my, um, apprentice, Clara," he said, indicating the girl who was now standing behind him patiently. All of the nervousness she had shown earlier was gone. "She helps me give the crowd a little nudge, warms them up a bit," he said, as though he were reading Ben's mind.

Clara performed a little curtsy and Ben nodded his head to her.

Percival looked at Ben warily for a moment.

"It's not every day you see a hill goblin this far into a human city," he said, speaking the words slowly and as nonchalantly as he could. He followed the statement with a casual, yet inquisitive stare.

Ben just shrugged.

The magician waited a little longer for a more in-depth response but when he realized that nothing was forthcoming, he just smiled and tipped his hat.

"Best of luck to you, kid. Perhaps we'll meet again someday!"

And with that, he and Clara disappeared into the long evening shadows.

6.

LAMP LIGHTING AND TRAIN WATCHING

Maribel's route was in a section just north of the heart of the city, in the Academy district, so named because it housed the city's great school of learning. It was a route that was much sought after by all lamplighters in the guild.

The professors used their non-teaching hours to work on research or to blow off steam at one of the nearby pubs, which were nothing at all like the pubs on the docks. The glasses were washed, the barkeeps didn't look like you were putting them out when you ordered something, and the alcohol wasn't nearly as watered down. The students, on the other hand, spent their nights studying in their rooms or conducting research of their own in the vast Academy library. The streets were therefore clean, quiet, and as safe as you could find in the middle of a city in the pre-night hours.

Maribel had told Ben that it had always been her desire to attend the Academy, but her father had other plans for her — plans that she had no interest in herself. Still, walking the streets every night in the middle of it all was, for her, a decent compensation. Ben could understand that, feeling that same draw to the area, if for completely different reasons. Maribel's hope was that one day she could save up enough money to be able to either pay for her own tuition or at least let out a room in the district, but room prices were steep and tuition was even steeper.

Ben and Maribel spent the next several hours lighting the lamps of the district. She showed Ben how she used the pole to first open the glass door on the lamp and then twist the handle to turn the gas flow on. Then she tipped it up slightly so that the hooked end, called a by-pass, touched the gas inside and ignited the flame, bringing the lamp and the area around it to life in a soft flickering glow.

After every lamp had been lit, leaving the district awash in light under the now, full-dark sky, they ended their night sitting at Union Station, a train depot that had been constructed less than a decade ago. Ben couldn't stop staring at the ceiling, which was sixty-five feet high, barrel-vaulted, and from which hung an immense wrought iron chandelier with more light bulbs than he could count.

He marveled at the number of trains coming and going, each full of travelers going about their lives. He couldn't help but wonder if the humans fully appreciated the freedom and privileges they possessed.

Every evening thereafter, before his night watch began, Ben returned to the train station. On some nights, Maribel joined him after her rounds, bringing with her pastries from the nearby bakery and hot coffee. Until she arrived, though, Ben sat in a far corner, out of the way of the crowds, where he could go unnoticed and gaze in fascination at the many steam locomotives coming and going from the giant depot. He fantasized about sneaking over and jumping onto one of the cars, allowing it to take him wherever it willed, perhaps to a place where goblins and humans co-existed as equals, if such a place even existed. Then he would inevitably think of Maribel, as he did so often throughout the course of the day, and he would settle back into his seat.

❧ ❧ ❧

Two and a half months passed in this way and it was now the 21st of December, just four days before Christmas. As goblins do not celebrate Christmas, he had never experienced the holiday firsthand, but he had read much about it. In his mind, he conjured up images of the March sisters celebrating the return of their father from the war, just in time for the holiday. He saw Ebenezer Scrooge gaily running around London with a fresh perspective on life. He wondered if this Christmas, now that there was someone in his life whom he actually cared for and cared for him in return, would be anything like those joyous fictional holidays.

As if summoned by the thought of her, Maribel appeared at his shoulder with a handful of raspberry tarts and two cups of coffee.

"Anything interesting tonight?" she asked, handing Ben his share of the food.

Ben shrugged. "Not really. I just like

watching. It relaxes me."

Maribel ate her tart and leaned back, yawning and stretching. After a moment, Ben felt her eyes on him and he turned to her.

"What's wrong?"

"It's funny, but you don't look like any of the pictures of goblins that I've ever seen," said Maribel.

"Really? How did they look?"

"Well, I suppose still sort of like yourself, just exaggerated a bit. Longer ears, larger nose, oh, and razor-sharp teeth of course, though I suppose that part was added for dramatic effect."

Ben smiled benignly. "Honest mistake, I guess."

Maribel laughed.

"I wouldn't be so forgiving if someone drew a picture of me like that!" she said. "I suppose it's just human nature to vilify what we don't understand."

"You have to admit, though," said Ben, "goblins aren't exactly innocent bystanders."

Maribel shrugged. "No, I suppose not, but you're living proof that not all goblins are bad."

"Just all but one," said Ben with a hint of sadness in his tone.

"What about your family?" she asked. "What are they like?"

"Not like me, that's for sure."

Maribel frowned. "Surely, they miss you, though?"

"I wouldn't count on it," Ben scoffed. "To my brothers, I was nothing more than a training dummy to test their skills on, and to my father, I was barely alive."

"And your mother?"

Ben shook his head. "My mother died giving birth to me."

Maribel put a hand on his shoulder, and the comfort of it drove some of his sadness away.

"It's okay," he said. "Honestly, I'm counting

on them not missing me. I'd rather die than go back to them."

They sat in silence for a while and had just finished their coffees when apparently Maribel couldn't handle the quiet any longer.

"So, tell me something I don't know about goblins," she said.

Ben was slightly taken off guard by the question and had to think about it for a moment.

"Well, we love to tell stories," he offered.

Maribel smiled and nodded.

"That one I could have guessed," she said, "with as much reading as you do. What else? There has to be something. Something that no other human would know."

Ben knew exactly what would satisfy her curiosity, and he also knew that it was absolutely forbidden for any goblin to divulge that particular bit of information. He weighed his options carefully. The look on Maribel's face — one of eagerness, inquisitiveness, and as with every look she gave him, kindness — ultimately won him over.

"Alright, but you have to promise that you won't tell a soul. I'd be flayed alive if any goblin knew that I told this to a human."

Maribel's eyes widened and she leaned forward conspiratorially. "Cross my heart," she said.

Ben looked at her curiously.

"It means I promise."

Nodding his understanding, he said, "Right, well, okay. The greatest secret of the goblin race that no other human in the world knows . . ." He paused and wiped his brow. A cold sweat broke out across his skin at the mere prospect of betraying his race so fully.

Maribel took his hands. "You don't have to tell me," she said. "I didn't mean to cause you such anxiety."

Ben shook his head. "No, I want to. It may

actually be useful to you someday if you continue to spend time with me."

He took a deep breath and let it out on a long sigh. "Alright, goblins have the ability, well, we can create illusions."

Maribel frowned. "I don't think I understand."

Ben gestured to the train station around them. "We, well not me, I've never really had the knack for it, but other goblins can create grand illusions; make you see things that aren't really there. For example, we could be sitting out in the middle of the forest but a goblin who knew what they were doing could make it seem like we were sitting in the middle of a train station and we would believe it, at least until the moment that something happened that shouldn't, you know, something out of place, like an owl flying through a train or someone's head. That would break our sense of belief and, in turn, the illusion."

"That's incredible," whispered Maribel, who obviously felt the weight of the profound secret that she now held.

Ben shrugged. "It is. I always wished I could do it, too, but I could just never seem to get it right."

Maribel squeezed his hands tighter. "You've gotten a lot of other things right that the rest of your race could learn from."

Ben smiled and when he felt the hot prickle of tears welling up in the corner of his eyes, he turned his head, trying to blink them away before she saw. That was when he noticed two things.

The first was Jacob, the guild member who had scolded him so severely months before and seemed to have such disdain for goblins. He was walking toward them and, for a moment, Ben thought he had seen them. Then he realized that Jacob wasn't so much walking toward them as he was walking away from the incident unfolding behind him.

Several more people followed Jacob's lead, only these people weren't walking, they were running, and the looks on their faces were terror personified. Ben searched for the source of their terror and a few seconds later, he realized what they were running from and, suddenly, he felt like running, too.

7.
GOBLINS ON A TRAIN

"What's wrong?" asked Maribel.

She had been looking at Ben and not at the scene below. She had yet to see the pack of at least ten goblins that had de-boarded a cargo train and was now slicing through the hordes of humans like sharks through water. A particularly loud scream pierced the air, causing Ben to flinch and Maribel to immediately leap to her feet.

"We have to go," she said to Ben, who sat rooted to the spot in fear. "We have to go now!"

She grabbed his arm and pulled his small frame upward. They dropped their empty cups and ran as fast as they could to the nearest exit. Up ahead, Ben spotted Jacob, who had stopped walking and was now watching the unfolding chaos. He didn't seem to notice them and Ben would have crashed right into him had a strong, green hand not grabbed hold of Ben's arm and yanked him in the opposite direction.

Ben tried to shout to Maribel but no sound escaped his lips. He tried to move but his legs were numbed. He could do nothing but allow himself to be dragged away from the only person in the world whom he cared about.

❖ ❖ ❖

It took Maribel just a second too late to realize Ben wasn't beside her anymore. She whirled around and began to run after him when a hand grabbed her arm. She turned to see who had hold of her.

"Jacob? What are you doing?" she asked.

"It's not safe here. We have to go," he said, pulling her toward the exit.

She shook her head and tried to free her arm, but his grip was too tight.

"Let go of me! They've got Ben! Jacob, let go!"

Jacob's grip tightened and he pulled on her harder.

"Forget the goblin and save yourself."

"No!"

Maribel took Jacob's arm with her free hand, twisting it so that his grip instantly broke and he squirmed in pain. She held his arm behind his back for a second longer.

"Don't try to stop me again," she said and then released him.

She turned and ran as fast as she could in the direction of Ben's captors. The goblins, though, had boarded another train. By the time she reached it, the train was halfway out of the station, nearly fifty yards down the track.

She pursued on foot, following the tracks as they exited the station and headed out of the city. Her legs were beginning to tire as the adrenaline wore off, and she stopped to catch her breath. It was then that she noticed that she was being followed.

Maribel turned to see Jacob catching up behind her, breathing heavily.

"What . . . in the hell . . . are you doing?" he asked her in between gasps.

She took a deep breath herself and then leaned over, her hands resting on her knees.

"Following my friend."

Jacob shook his head and turned his back to her, hands on his hips.

"He's a goblin, you know."

Maribel laughed. She couldn't help herself. "Really? Is that why he's short and green?"

"How can you so casually befriend a goblin?" Jacob asked without turning around.

Maribel stood up and frowned. "How can

you so casually disregard him as just another goblin? If you took a moment to get to know him, you'd realize he's nothing like the rest of them."

Jacob turned then and his face was a mask of irritation.

"I don't care if he's a little less ruthless than other goblins, he's still a goblin, and goblins are a scourge on this earth. They steal from us, they burn our houses, they kill our friends and family. No goblin deserves a moment of my time."

Maribel started to argue but realized it was pointless. She just sighed, shook her head, and began to follow the train tracks once more.

"You know you can't save him," Jacob shouted after her. "What good can you do against a horde of goblins?"

"I can try," she replied, not turning back. "And Ben says it's not a horde of goblins but a malignity of goblins, which I don't think is much better, but oh well."

Jacob scoffed. "His family won't give him up so easily."

These words made her turn to face him again. "How do you know they're his family?"

Jacob hesitated, perhaps a bit too long, and then shrugged. "Who else would care enough about that green-skinned little monster to pull the stunt they pulled to get him?"

Maribel stared at Jacob for a few breaths more and then returned to her pursuit.

An hour or so passed, the moon was full, high in the night sky, and it had begun to snow lightly. Jacob was still following her, she could hear the crunch of his footsteps on the gravel and snow. They had left the city behind at least half an hour before. They were now headed south and the tracks were about to enter a copse of trees. Maribel knew that this was just the beginning of what would be a very hilly and woodsy trek.

She stopped for another break and walked up to Jacob.

"I don't know why you're still following me. You obviously don't care about Ben."

Jacob looked miserable. It was absolutely freezing out and he had lost his coat and scarf, most likely in his initial pursuit of her. His face was filthy and he was sweating, despite the cold.

"You're a guild member. I can't lose two in one night. I plan on being guild master someday."

"Hmpf," she snorted. "I'm guessing no more goblins get hired then."

He said nothing in reply and she surveyed him cautiously.

"Fine, follow me if you want, but if you try to stop me from helping him, I'll break your arm next time. I don't need some boy trying to be chivalrous holding me back. As you saw, I'm capable of looking out for myself."

Jacob nodded in agreement and held up his hands. "Fine," he muttered.

"Fine."

They began walking again and Maribel's thoughts turned back to her purpose. Jacob was undoubtedly right. Those goblins had to be Ben's family. At that moment, all she could think of were the words that Ben had spoken not long before.

I'd rather die than go back to them.

8.

A WINTER'S TALE

Ben awoke to the smells of burning wood, cooking meat, and the unmistakable aroma of goblins. The first two would have been pleasant enough under normal circumstances, but the latter made his blood run cold.

Not that there was anything particularly offensive about the smell of goblins. It was a scent so subtle that no human would have ever picked it up. But its sudden re-emergence into Ben's life made it noticeable and dreaded.

They were no longer moving, that was for

sure. He remembered clearly when they jumped from the open door of the train car. He had hit his head on a tree and it had knocked him out stone cold. The ground beneath him now was soft and he wondered how far they had traveled from the track.

He opened his eyes to find a scene much like he had imagined. A large fire crackled not ten feet from where he lay. His eldest brother — who else would have braved a plan as reckless as that — stood turning the spit, where a headless pig was roasting. The other nine goblins were either sitting around casually, speaking in low tones, or lying back with their eyes closed. He could hear the soft trickle of a stream in the distance, not loud enough for the Mississippi. It hardly mattered where they were, though; he knew exactly where they were taking him.

To his surprise, he saw that he was not bound in any way. In fact, no one was paying any attention to him at all. Despite this, he knew any attempt at escape would only add to his discomfort. At least now, he didn't have any arrows protruding from his back.

"A tale!" one of the goblins called in a boisterous voice.

Ben jumped at the sudden noise and soon other voices concurred with the first's suggestion.

"A tale! A tale!" they shouted, stomping their feet in unison.

His brother Killan smiled and bowed his head in assent. He released the spit and motioned for another to take his place.

"Hmm," he said, folding his arms and rubbing his chin in concentration. "Very well, I have just the winter's tale for a cold night such as this. It is called *The Tale of the Blacksmith and the Lordling*."

❊ ❊ ❊

There was once a goblin blacksmith by the

name of Brandt. He was renowned far and wide for his great skill, and it was said that he crafted the finest steel that gold could buy.

One winter's day, the spoiled son of a human lord visited the smith and asked if he would forge for him a sword unmatched by any other in the world. Like today, it wasn't at all common then for a human to do business with a goblin, and so Brandt rejected the request. However, the lordling offered the goblin twenty gold coins as payment.

Knowing full well that the reward for his services was far more than he had ever earned before, Brandt agreed and told the lordling to return in one month.

One month came and went, and the lordling returned to the goblin's forge. Brandt held out the sword and the lordling marveled at its beauty. Truly this was a sword unmatched by any other in the world. The goblin then held out his hand and asked for his promised payment of twenty gold coins, but the lordling only scoffed and tossed five coins on the counter.

"It's more than a goblin deserves," he said and with no more explanation than that, he turned and left.

When he arrived home to his father's manor, he unsheathed his newest prize and admired it. It was perfect in all ways, though the longer he held it, the colder the hilt grew. As it was the middle of winter and he had just ridden five miles on horseback in the chill air, he thought nothing of it. He brought it inside and set it near the hearth where a crackling fire sat in the grate. Then he strode off to attend his dinner.

When he returned an hour later, however, he found the sword nearly completely melted, sitting in a puddle of water. Upon seeing this, the illusion that had been placed on the sword was broken to reveal nothing more than what had been an overlarge icicle.

Furious at being deceived, the lordling

returned to the forge the next day, demanding the true sword. Brandt chuckled and apologized for his little trick. He then produced another sword, identical in all ways to the previous one. The lordling touched the hilt and held it for a while, and when it did not grow cold under his touch, he smiled and sheathed the sword.

Once more, the goblin held out his hand and asked for the payment he had been promised, but, once again, the lordling threw only five coins on the counter and left.

When he returned home, he placed the sword by the hearth again and once more set off for his dinner. When he returned, the carpet upon which the tip of the sword had been resting was burning rapidly, and a great hole had been torn through it. Upon seeing this, the illusion was broken and in the sword's place was a hot poker that was still bright orange at its tip.

Once again, the lordling returned to the forge and demanded the true sword and, once again, the goblin chuckled at his trickery and produced a third sword, identical in all ways to the first two. He held it aloft as the lordling touched the hilt and then the tip, and when he was satisfied, Brandt offered to sheath it for him.

Then, as before, he held out his hand and asked for the payment he had been promised. The lordling looked enraged at having been deceived twice already, but he threw another five coins on the counter and left.

When he arrived home, he withdrew his sword and took a practice swing but at that same moment, a strong gale blew and took hold of the sword, blowing it away on the wind. As it disappeared, the lordling could see the sword transform into a long peacock feather.

For the fourth and final time, the lordling returned to the forge and before the goblin could even smile, the lordling slammed five more gold coins on the counter.

"There, twenty gold coins, as promised," he snarled. "Now give me my sword!"

Brandt did not chuckle but merely nodded and reached under the counter, pulling out a fourth sword. He held it out but pulled back slightly when the lordling reached for it.

"Before I hand this over, you must swear to me that this blade will never be used against goblin flesh."

The lordling looked annoyed but nodded his agreement. He then took the sword and set off for home.

He was nearly there, just on the edge of the forest that surrounded his ancestral estate, when he was ambushed by masked thieves dressed all in black. Their small statures and deft movements revealed them to be goblins.

They struck at his horse first, taking down the beast with a flurry of arrows. Surrounded and outnumbered, the lordling drew the only weapon he possessed, his promise all too quickly forgotten.

The nearest goblin rushed at him. He parried the blow and sent his riposte aimed directly at his attacker's chest. However, the moment that his sword touched goblin flesh, it gave a violent shudder and transfigured itself into a black snake. The snake recoiled and lunged at the lordling's throat and in a matter of seconds, the lordling was laying on the ground, gasping his final breaths.

His last vision before the darkness overtook him was of one of the goblin thieves standing over him, his mask now removed. Perhaps it was simply the poison or his own prejudice clouding his mind, but the lordling would have sworn that he glimpsed the face of the blacksmith.

✤ ✤ ✤

"The end," Killan said with a flourish and a

bow.

The other goblins guffawed and cheered riotously.

"'A sad tale's best for winter,'" whispered Ben, so softly that only he could hear. Shakespeare's words only brought him some slight comfort in that moment.

He sat up and the sound caused his brother's eyes to move quickly to him. Killan excused himself from the others and came to sit next to Ben.

"You took quite the tumble, little brother."

Ben looked down and said nothing.

His brother smiled. "It's good to see you again."

"Is it?" Ben looked up in surprise at these words, genuinely curious.

Killan, so named after one of the great goblin heroes, laughed briefly and patted Ben on the back. The touch sent a chill up Ben's spine.

"In a way, yes. After all, I have been

searching for you these past three months. Our other brothers were all sent out first but when their searches proved fruitless, father assigned me to the task.

"So, I suppose a more accurate answer would be yes and no. Yes, it is good to have found you and thus I am seeing you, but, no, I'm not necessarily happy to partake in your company."

Just like a goblin, Ben thought, using thirty words when three would do.

He didn't dare say this aloud.

"I'm surprised anyone noticed I was gone," said Ben.

His brother shrugged. "We didn't for a while but even the most egregious pest can become noticed by its absence. Quite brave of you, actually. Personally, I wouldn't have thought you had it in you."

"Thanks," said Ben, not quite sure whether this was a compliment.

"Brave, yes, but quite foolish. You do know the penalty for treason, don't you?"

Ben felt a chill of panic run through him. How could they have known what he'd told Maribel only hours before? No, they couldn't know.

"I haven't committed treason," said Ben. "I just left a place where I wasn't wanted."

Killan brushed the argument aside. "Desertion and treason are synonymous. One leads to the other. Deserters spill secrets which is in turn . . . treason."

Ben felt the sweat beading up on his forehead and knew that Killan would notice.

"Tsk, tsk, calm down, little brother," said Killan, patting his shoulder again. "Unluckily for you, deserters are never trusted, and since you are a deserter . . . . You violated your covenant to your own kind and abandoned your family."

"Well, that's convenient for you," Ben said

quietly.

His brother's hand flew unseen and cracked Ben across the face.

Killan's entire facial expression changed. The mask of calm politeness had been replaced by his true face — one of pure rage.

"You would be wise not to anger me any more than I already am. I've wasted too much of my time already seeking out your pathetic carcass, time that could have been spent doing much more important things, which considering my prey, would be just about anything else. You will be silent from henceforth unless you are spoken to."

He began to walk away but turned back and said, in a gentler tone, which was perhaps more frightening, "Sleep well, brother. Know that every goblin here is as angered and frustrated as I am, and though we have been instructed to bring you back alive, I wouldn't begrudge anyone here if they took out their frustration on your miserable hide while you slept."

With that, he walked away, leaving Ben completely speechless.

9.

PURSUIT

Signs of the morning's imminent arrival were becoming more apparent when Maribel stopped. They hadn't had a break in hours and having feeling in her legs was a distant memory. She was lucky that she had decided to wear her warmest coat that night. The day before had been mild by December standards so she had almost gone with her usual, standard-issue guild jacket. She wasn't actually sure what made her change her mind. Not that it mattered now. All that mattered was that she had been able to walk all night in the frigid air and, to her knowledge, had not contracted frostbite on any of her appendages.

The sound of waking birds coincided with the lightening of the sky from black to dark blue. But it wasn't the sky that concerned her at that moment. She was looking down at the ground on the side of the tracks, where her focus had been for the last several hours. Finally, she had found what she hoped she would find.

"What does this look like to you?" she called back to Jacob, who was only a few paces behind.

Jacob caught her up and studied the area where she was looking. The gravel on the side of the tracks had obviously been disturbed recently. It was noticeably spread farther away than anywhere else along the line. In addition, several of the scrub bushes that dotted the landscape had been smashed and broken.

"Looks like either a herd of cattle crossed the tracks here on a stampede or a group . . . sorry, a malignity of goblins jumped out of a moving train."

Maribel would have smiled had her numbed face worked properly.

"That's what I thought, too," she said. "Now if only we could figure out which direction they headed from here."

Jacob surveyed the area for several minutes and then returned to her.

"They went that way," he said confidently, pointing off to the south.

"Are you sure?

He nodded. "Yes, they didn't take care to hide their tracks. What fools would actually care to follow them?"

Maribel scowled at him but went to look for the tracks. When she was confident in Jacob's assessment, she began to follow the footsteps of the goblins. Jacob shook his head and sighed but followed without a word of protest.

The footprints led deeper into the woods, where the coming sun hardly penetrated. They walked in silence for a while, Maribel watching both the tracks and the distant trees ahead of her. She had a vision of herself so intent on keeping an eye on the footprints that she walked straight into a waiting goblin. That was not a mistake she was eager to make.

"Good job finding the tracks," said Maribel in a hushed voice. "I might have missed them entirely."

Jacob shrugged but didn't reply.

"Are you a hunter?" she asked.

"I used to go with my father when I was a kid," he replied, "but that was a while ago."

"Hmm."

"What?" asked Jacob.

"Well, it's just that I've never heard you say anything about your own life. For all I know, you're married, have a houseful of kids, and an overbearing mother-in-law."

Jacob snickered. "None of the above," he said.

Maribel laughed. "Okay, no wife or kids. What about siblings?"

Jacob said nothing for a while and the silence that followed was full of unexpected tension. At last, he said, "I don't really like to discuss myself, if that's alright."

He said it with such an air of finality that Maribel didn't bother prodding him.

They continued to follow the tracks on the ground as the sun rose higher in the sky. While the added light helped them see for greater distances, they were all too aware that the reverse was also true, and they did their best to not draw any unwanted attention their way.

❈ ❈ ❈

Ben's eyes opened when a boot kicked him squarely in the ribs, drawing out his breath rapidly and doubling him over. Though his eyes had been closed, he had never actually fallen asleep. His brother's words had haunted him and he kept a constant watch on all of the other goblins. He had only rested his eyes for a moment when the painful wake-up call had arrived.

"Up, little brother," said Killan, offering Ben a hand. "We have much walking ahead of us today. I hope you rested well."

Ben ignored the proffered help and stood on his own. Killan smirked.

"Your friends aren't far behind. We'll have to make haste lest they overtake us."

Ben's head jerked up and he stared incredulously at his brother, whose smile only widened.

"Ah, so you didn't know?" he asked mockingly. "I began to sense their presence a few hours ago. Our scouts spotted them about a mile back. I must say, for humans, I'm a bit impressed. And I'm a little disappointed you didn't sense them as well."

Ben said nothing in response.

"You've lived among humans too long, little brother," Killan goaded. "Your senses have dulled to their level."

Still too astonished at the idea of anyone actually coming after him, Ben once again didn't rise to his brother's baiting. Surely Killan was wrong.

"Who are they?" he asked, taking a chance that his brother wouldn't mind the unsolicited question.

"One male and one female. They both wear the same human rags that you do."

Maribel, it had to be her. Who else would even lift a finger for him? But who was the man? If he wore the same clothes as he and Maribel, then he must be a guild member. She must have convinced someone to help her. There was no one else he knew that would willingly help him. And now that he thought about it, he was happy that Killan knew about them. If the goblins increased their speed, they would surely outpace her. He hoped she would turn back once it was obvious that they wouldn't be able to overtake them.

"Of course," Killan said, cutting into Ben's thoughts, "we will be splitting up. Half of our party will continue onward home; the rest will circle back around them. They'll make sure that they never reach Jotunfell."

"No!" shouted Ben, suddenly terrified and enraged. "Just leave them alone! You have me, don't hurt them!"

Again, his brother's fist came swiftly and without warning. This time it was followed by another series of blows that sent Ben careening back to the ground, cracking his head on a log in the process. Killan proceeded to kick his chest and stomach repeatedly until Ben had to gasp for breath and he knew that he was going to be beaten to death.

The blows ceased as abruptly as they had began. Ben squeezed his eyes closed and used every fiber of energy left in his weary, beaten body to fight for breath.

He felt the dark of unconsciousness creeping in but before it did, his brother's voice appeared in his ear.

"We all make our own choices in life, brother, and they have made theirs. But fear not, I'll be sure their bodies are brought to the city so that you can say your goodbyes before joining them."

10.

AMBUSH

When Ben finally came to, the first thing he noticed was his shoulders aching. He quickly realized the cause when he saw the two burly goblins on each side of him, clasping his arms and dragging him roughly between them.

The second thing he noticed was how thirsty he was. He hadn't had a drink of anything since the coffee the night before. How he longed to be back there now. One day ago, he felt as safe and secure as a goblin living in a human city could feel. It had been a year since he had left

Jotunfell. He had surely thought that no one would still be looking for him. And yet, here he was, literally being dragged back to that hated, hateful city at the mercy of his cruelest brother.

He tried to ask for water but his throat was too dry to speak. Killan, however, noticed that he was awake and he motioned for the group to stop.

"I hesitate to give this to you," Killan said as he loosened the water pouch from his belt. "Dry mouths don't speak treacherous sympathies.

"However," he added, jabbing his finger into a bruise on Ben's cheek, which caused the captive goblin to flinch with a sharp burst of pain, "I think you've learned your lesson."

He motioned for the goblins holding Ben to release him. His numbed legs buckled at the sudden weight and he crumpled to the ground.

Killan leaned over him and offered the water. Ben took it and drank slowly. The cool liquid felt life-giving as it worked its way down his throat.

"Thank you," he croaked when he had drunk his fill.

Killan re-attached the pouch and nodded. The burly goblins took hold of Ben again but he waved them off, determined to walk on his own.

They walked all day, stopping only momentarily for short meals of stale bread and salted jerky. As the sun dropped below the horizon, Killan called for an abrupt stop.

"What is it?" asked one of the goblins who had drug Ben earlier.

"Shhh," said Killan in a low whisper. "We're being watched."

A wave of fear swept over Ben. Maribel had caught up to them. Somehow, she and whoever accompanied her had managed to outpace a troupe of goblins moving rapidly through familiar woods, and now they would be killed for their efforts.

However, he then heard a rustling noise in the trees nearby. And it was quickly followed by another and then another. His head swung around, staring into the trees when he realized that they were completely surrounded. He had just begun to wonder who they were when the first arrow fell.

※ ※ ※

Maribel and Jacob heard a high-pitched scream that turned their blood cold merely at the sound of it. Definitely a goblin. They ran as fast as they could in the direction of the sound, pulling up short as they reached the edge of a clearing. Up ahead, a battle was taking place, or, rather, a skirmish, for there were not nearly enough participants for it to be classified as a full-on battle.

Green-skinned goblins with daggers and short swords traded blows with a small host of light- and dark-skinned humans. At first it wasn't clear who was winning. It appeared that equal of their numbers lay dead upon the ground. Soon, however, the smaller and outnumbered goblins showed the ferocity that their race was feared for as they began to overtake their ambushers.

Maribel scanned the chaotic crowd. It only took a few moments before she noticed Ben huddled behind a tree, doing his best to stay away from the fighting.

"Come on!" shouted Maribel over the din of noise coming from the clearing. She grabbed Jacob's arm and pulled him after her.

They skirted around the clearing, staying out of sight until they reached Ben, who only saw her coming at the last moment before she lunged onto him, pulling him into a tight embrace.

"I thought I'd never see you again," she whispered in his ear.

Ben was speechless and before he could force himself to respond, she had taken his arm and led him away.

❋ ❋ ❋

With the sound of fighting at their heels, they ran back in the direction from which they had come. Ben tripped a few times but jumped up immediately and rejoined the race. Their hearts were near to bursting in their chests with effort and, for the briefest of seconds, it seemed like they might actually escape. And that's when the silence fell.

The sounds of steel against steel, of goblins screaming, and of humans screaming, all came to a sudden, deafening halt. The change was so unexpected that it forced Maribel, Ben, and Jacob to slow and look behind them. For a moment, there was nothing but the wind through the leaves. One moment more and they were met with a terrifying sight.

Goblins hurtled toward them, racing so swiftly and so quietly across the earth, slipping between trees and bushes, that they seemed like apparitions. No sounds did they make — not the snapping of sticks or the crunching of leaves. Maribel shouted something that brought life back to their legs momentarily and they continued to run, though they all knew in their hearts that it was pointless.

They spent so much time looking back that they didn't notice the other half of the goblin party that had circled back around behind them.

11.

THE WILES OF A GOBLIN

"Please, don't hurt her."

Jacob and Killan stood alone among the trees. Ben and Maribel had already been taken back to camp, where the surviving goblins were busy looting their ambushers' lifeless bodies. Killan was enjoying this. He loved holding all the power, especially over a human. He took his time responding, relishing every moment of Jacob's fear.

"That wasn't part of the deal," Killan said at last. "We agreed that in exchange for you telling me where to find my brother, I would take him off your hands without harming anyone in the city. I held up my end of the bargain. And as you can see . . ."

He held up his arms and looked around the thick woods. ". . . We are no longer in the city. Our bargain is at an end. I made no promises about anyone that pursued us."

Jacob shook his head. "I know, I tried to stop her, but she was relentless. Just let her go and I promise she won't bother you again."

Killan scoffed. "And you've done such a fine job of controlling her thus far."

Killan turned and took a deep breath, enjoying the cool evening air filling his lungs. "I'm in a good mood," he said without facing Jacob. "I've killed many humans already tonight, so I will stay my dagger for now."

"Thank you, thank . . ." Jacob began but the goblin cut him off.

"We'll let my father decide what is to become

of you humans."

Jacob's knees buckled and he had to hold on to a nearby tree to steady himself.

"Your . . . your father? You're taking us to Jotunfell?"

Killan turned back to the human and smiled wide at the unmitigated fear on his face, savored it. Then he left him behind without another word.

❖ ❖ ❖

Back at the newly-erected campsite, Ben and Maribel were tied together, back-to-back. No one was really paying much attention to them, too busy were they with their looting.

"Who do you think they were?" asked Maribel quietly.

"Goblin hunters, I would imagine," answered Ben. "I've never seen them before, but I've heard plenty of stories about them."

"Goblin hunters," repeated Maribel. "If only they would have won, we'd be free right now."

"*You* would be free," interjected a new voice. Killan casually strolled to where they were seated and sat down so that they both could see him.

"My brother, on the other hand, would have been killed the moment they saw him, without a word."

"You don't know that," argued Maribel. "I would have told them . . ."

"You wouldn't have been given the chance. Trust me, my dear, I've been killing goblin hunters as long as I can remember. They never hesitate when a goblin is in sight, never."

Maribel fell silent.

"You should be happy it was us that won. If those wretched humans had proved victorious, I doubt you would have made it through the night unscathed. Goblin hunters are renowned for their lustfulness. It's a lonely life, spending nearly all of your time in the wilderness with no companionship but the man beside you."

"And I'm supposed to believe you're any different?" she retorted.

"Ha!" laughed Killan. He spat on the ground at her feet. "I already believe you to be mentally unbalanced for having followed us this far, but you would have to be truly mad if you thought, for even an instant, that I or any other goblin would ever have any desire for a pale human female."

"Please just let her go, you have me, she's nothing to you," pleaded Ben.

Killan looked at his brother severely. "I've already had this conversation with you, and I never repeat myself. We'll sleep here for the night and first thing in the morning, we set off for home. Father will decide your fates."

❀ ❀ ❀

The first rays of dawn were peering over the horizon when the goblins and their captives set off on the final leg of their journey.

The two humans and their goblin

companion, not being allowed near the fire, had gotten little sleep as the night had turned bitterly cold.

They were kept separated, a pair of goblins between each captive, with Ben leading the way. Killan wanted his brother to be the first of their party seen upon entering the gates of Jotunfell. Being the eldest son and his father's heir, he technically had nothing to gain from his victory. But the ability to gloat and say that he had succeeded where all his siblings had failed was reward enough.

They walked all morning and around midday, it began to snow again. It was soon up to the goblins' knees and Killan considered stopping until it receded, but catching sight of the lights of his city in the distance spurred him onward. His moment of glory was at hand.

❊ ❊ ❊

When Ben saw the gates of Jotunfell, the full reality of his situation finally overwhelmed him.

Up until that point, it had almost seemed as if it were just a bad dream, as though he was watching it happen to someone else and then he would awake, back in the lighthouse, in the only place where he had ever truly felt at home. Seeing this dreaded place again after a year of being gone made it all too real. For truly the first time, he began to fear the looming confrontation with his father.

His father's reputation and icy demeanor had always made Ben nervous when he had been thrust into his company. He knew he probably wouldn't survive their next meeting and yet he realized that it was not himself he was worried for.

❖ ❖ ❖

Maribel heard the roar of the crowds before the doors of the city had even been opened. It was unmistakably hostile and it made her muscles involuntarily convulse.

As they drew near, the large gates of the

walled city creaked open and thousands of goblins — more than she had ever seen at once — instantly came into view. They lined the streets, hung out of open windows, and sat atop rooftops. The obvious hatred they showed for her and Jacob made her blood run cold.

She had heard the leader of their goblin captors refer to Ben as a traitor and now she saw firsthand just how big a crime that was in their society.

❖ ❖ ❖

Ben glanced back at Maribel and Jacob and imagined what they were seeing and hearing. He let what small amount of control over his sense of *kenna* he possessed slip slightly and thousands of shouting, angry goblins instantly filled the streets. Even though he knew it wasn't real, the illusion was frightening nonetheless.

He brought his mental guard back up and the streets returned to their normal state. This illusion was the biggest secret of the goblins and their greatest strength.

They had not nearly the numbers that the humans believed they did. In fact, the hill goblins who inhabited this part of the world were practically an endangered race of beings. This was a chief reason why they took desertion so seriously and why a goblin born such as Ben was so disappointing. Every goblin birth was celebrated and to be born different was seen only as a wasted opportunity.

They passed through the market square where only a handful of carts and stalls stood empty. Goblins conducted their business in the morning and by high noon, the large square was abandoned. This was partly because of the flights of fancies of the merchants, but it was also a law, just another part of the rigid schedule that goblin life was built around.

As they made their way through the city, they passed several goblins wearing the traditional light-weight robes of their race, each dyed a different color depending on the owner's trade or status. Goblins wearing blue robes were the main practitioners of the illusory arts, and thus they all had their noses stuck into books and paid the passing party no mind. Those in red and green were the builders and engineers. It was a goblin wearing purple robes, the color of the aristocracy, who first noticed them. As they approached, he wrinkled up his nose. His eyes scanned the group and when they fell upon the two humans, they narrowed. He held a hand up to his face, covering his nose before turning abruptly around and heading back in the direction from whence he had come.

They were led promptly to the Hob's Keep, which with true goblin efficiency, was a direct path from the city gates with no turns. Jotunfell itself was built in a perfect grid with all buildings constructed with the same clay bricks, timber siding, steeply-pitched roofs, and cobblestone chimneys jutting out from their tops. The road itself was laid with the same cobblestone, packed so tightly and expertly that one couldn't feel any imbalance when walking over it.

As they reached the keep's gates, all the goblins in their party save for Killan were replaced by three of the Hob's personal guard. Their trek finally ended in what was obviously the Hob's throne room. He was not present at that moment but they were lined up and told to wait in silence. Killan disappeared through a side door and re-emerged a few minutes later, accompanied by an older goblin.

"Tamoren, the sixth of his name, Great Hob of Jotunfell," announced one of the guards in an official-sounding voice.

The Hob was shorter than the younger goblins but his gray-black hair was three times as long with a beard to match, all braided intricately with green stones woven throughout. The points of his ears had begun to curl inward with age, and they were decorated with many golden rings. He wore circular, golden rimmed, darkly-shaded glasses that let in no light and a long, crimson robe that drug along the ground. His movements were so precise and fluid that it almost appeared as though he were levitating.

Tamoren stopped in front of Ben and stared at his youngest son without saying a word. It took everything Ben had to not look away, but he refused to give his father the satisfaction of knowing just how frightened he was.

"Leave us," said Tamoren, in a voice much deeper than his stature would have suggested.

Killan and the Hob's guards exchanged glances. It was unclear to whom the Hob was addressing.

"Father?" asked Killan inquiringly.

"All of you but the captives," clarified Tamoren, and his tone left no room for doubt or argument.

Killan nodded and bowed and followed the guards out of the room. When they heard the door shut and the lock click into place, the old goblin's face changed.

He reached up and removed his glasses, revealing eyes that were the deep, peaceful green of the sea at dusk . . . Ben's eyes.

Then the Hob did something that none had ever seen a goblin do. He leaned forward and embraced his son.

12.

THE GREAT HOB OF JOTUNFELL

Ben had imagined this moment many times in the last two and a half days but in none of those scenarios did his father react in this way.

Tamoren leaned back but still held his son's shoulders.

"My son," he said in a choked voice.

"Father?" said Ben, more a question than a statement.

Tamoren wiped at his eyes and nodded, understanding his son's confusion too well.

"I think I have much to explain," he said,

"but not here."

He turned and motioned for the others to follow him back through the door from which he had entered the room.

Neither Ben, Maribel, nor Jacob moved an inch. Tamoren stopped in the doorway and turned back to them.

"I give you my word that no harm will come to you as long as you follow me. I can make no such promises as long as we remain here, so close to prying souls."

Ben and Maribel exchanged glances and finally Ben nodded as they silently agreed that they had limited options. Jacob said nothing but fell in behind them.

Tamoren led them through a chamber outfitted as a sitting room, complete with a fireplace, stiff-looking armchairs that appeared to have never been used, and several bookcases. At the opposite end of the room was another door, this one leading to a narrow staircase.

They ascended the stairs for some time and Maribel lost count of how many flights they had climbed. Finally, the stairs ended at a door, and Tamoren reached into his robe for a key, which he inserted into the keyhole.

"These are my personal chambers. We may speak freely here," said Tamoren as he hurried them inside and locked the door behind them.

Tamoren reached into his robes again and the others took a step back in alarm as he withdrew a long, crooked knife.

"Now, let's remove those restraints," he said, smiling as he watched their expressions change.

One by one, he quickly and efficiently cut all their bindings and then set the knife down on a nearby table.

Ben looked around the rooms. He had never been allowed in his father's private tower chambers. To his knowledge, no one had since his mother's passing two decades ago.

They were modestly decorated, not nearly as

elaborate as the rooms below. This first room had much of the same elements as the chamber they had passed through at the bottom of the stairs: a fireplace, armchairs, and bookcases, but these were much different. The fireplace had a warm fire crackling in the hearth and a pot of hot water resting on it that had just begun to whistle. The armchairs were not stiff but plushy and had several goblin-sized indentions in them where his father must have spent many hours sitting. The bookcases covered nearly every spare inch of wall space and were packed to overflowing with tomes of all sorts. However, one title, written in gold foil on the spine, stuck out to him from across the room . . . *The Man in the Iron Mask*.

"Father, you read Dumas?" Ben asked incredulous.

Tamoren turned instinctively, glancing at just the spot on his many bookcases where the Dumas books were resting.

"As do you," he said, smiling wryly. "Did you think you were the only one in Jotunfell who purchased human books?"

Ben shrugged. "I did, actually."

"Did you not find it curious that a bookseller would bring human books into a goblin city?"

"I . . ." Ben started. "Well, I never really thought about it."

"Of course, I told him that I only read them to study up on our enemy."

Ben was speechless.

Tamoren moved to the hearth and removed the steaming teapot. He poured the water into four cups before passing them around to his guests in silence.

At last, he sunk into a chair and motioned for everyone else to do the same. Hesitantly, they did.

"Now, you must have many questions, my son."

Ben looked down at his feet and then around

the room and then back to the goblin sitting before him. The father he thought he had known.

"Who *are* you?" he finally asked.

Tamoren nodded and it looked to Ben as though his father's eyes filled briefly with melancholy before he spoke.

"I was born different," he started. "Different from my parents, different from the children who were my playmates, different from the whole of our people. Sound familiar?"

He paused as Ben nodded.

"My father, your grandfather and the previous Hob, was a wise goblin. It was he who first began to use illusion not just as a trick but as a tactic, a weapon to strike fear in our enemies."

He snorted a derisive laugh.

"Our enemies. Those words I have spoken more times than I care to admit and yet they still ring as hollow to me now as they did the first time I uttered them.

"My mother, too, died in childbirth and my father, being older than he cared to admit, never took another wife. Thus, I was to be his only heir. He kept my abnormality a secret. These rooms were built for this exact purpose, to keep me far away from the rest of the city.

"He had a theory that my difference could be squashed out of me. The more I questioned our ideas, the more I was beaten. Eventually, I learned to lie and the beatings occurred less often. I realized that I held a role in our society that expected a certain thing from me, and I truly had no choice but to give it to them or my father would make my life nothing but torment and misery."

He shuddered, undoubtedly at the memory of his own father.

"I married out of duty. I sired seven children out of duty and out of a sort of resignation that this was my lot in life and I had no choice but to make the best of it. The night that you were born shook those ideas to their core. For here was another like me. How can someone be an anomaly if another exists in his image?"

He reached out and took Ben's hand in his. Ben's first reaction was to pull back but he stayed his hand.

"Unfortunately for you, I arrived too late. When I heard that there were complications, I went to your mother and though I admit that we never shared what could be considered 'love,' I held her hand and felt sorrow as I watched the life drain out of her.

"By the time I saw you and sensed your difference, the same difference that my father had sensed in me, too many others had sensed it as well and I knew that I had to tread lightly or expose myself in the process.

"I couldn't raise you as I had been but I also couldn't be kind to you. I couldn't be the father I wanted to be to you. For if I did, then my life's ruse would be at an end. So, I did what I thought was the kindest thing that I could do for you."

"You ignored me," interrupted Ben, now pulling his hand free. "You never talked to me, you wouldn't even acknowledge my presence. You made me feel even more worthless and alone than I already did."

Tamoren hung his head and closed his eyes.

"I am truly sorry, my son. What I did, I did because I thought it would be safest for all of us."

"You mean safest for you?" asked Maribel, who was sitting on the edge of her seat and leaning forward as far as she could without falling off.

"No," replied Tamoren, shaking his head fervently. "Safest for both of us. If I had been discovered, I would have been banished or killed and my entire family would have suffered the same fate."

"How do we know that you're not lying to us?" asked Maribel. "How do we know *this* isn't the ruse?"

"He's not lying," said Ben firmly. "I can sense his difference, I couldn't at first but I can now. How did you do that?"

Tamoren smiled sadly. "The one truly good thing your grandfather ever did for me," he said. "As I mentioned before, he was a pioneer in the usage of illusions and had a deep knowledge of our *kenna*. In his studies, he had discovered an old technique that scouts used to use, whereby they would disguise their true feelings so that they wouldn't be given away.

"Though I, like you, am not very skilled in the creating of illusions, my sense of *kenna* is strong and I was able to learn how to mask my feelings so effectively that no one could tell the difference between myself and any other goblin in the city."

"Why didn't you teach this to Ben then?"

asked Maribel.

Tamoren sighed deeply. "As I said, too many people already knew and besides, this technique takes some time to learn. If I had been noticed spending that much time alone with Ben, suspicions would have been aroused."

The room fell quiet as everyone absorbed the shocking information that had been shared.

"So, what happens to us now?" asked Ben, breaking the silence.

"Now, I help you cheat death."

Tamoren stood and walked to the large window on the opposite side of the room. The window looked out over the untouched hills and forests that surrounded the goblin stronghold. There were no other houses in sight.

Tamoren opened a cupboard and pulled out three folded pieces of silver cloth. He unfolded them and handed one to Ben, Maribel, and

Jacob in turn.

"Goblin wings," said Ben stunned. "I always wanted to use them but . . ."

"I never allowed it," finished Tamoren, "until now."

He unlatched the window lock and pushed the glass open.

"Use them and get far away as fast as you can. We feast tonight to celebrate Killan's successful return, so there will be no goblins outside the city walls to spy you."

"But wait, I still have more questions," said Ben. "Will we ever speak again?"

Tamoren smiled wider than he had yet shown and approached his son.

"Of course, my Benevolent, but we will need to be cautious."

"Benevolent?" asked Maribel.

Tamoren nodded. "My son's true name." He turned his eyes back to Ben and took a firm hold on his shoulders.

"I want you to remember something for me. With her dying breath, your mother named you Benevolent so that nobody would forget *what* you are. I named you Benevolent so that you would not forget *who* you are."

Ben began to feel the hot prickle of tears coming on.

"Go now," said Tamoren. "I will make the first contact. We will speak again very soon."

"What about Killan? What will you tell him?"

Tamoren smirked. "Don't worry, I'll come up with something. I'm used to lying to them by now."

Tamoren pulled his son to him and they embraced. This time, Ben reciprocated the gesture.

"Goodbye, Father. I'm glad to finally know you."

"Goodbye, my son. I'm glad to finally be known."

13.

THE TRAITOR REVEALED

It was decided that Ben would go first. If there were any goblins where they landed, he would be in the least amount of danger, at least as long as they didn't recognize him. When he landed safely and signaled back that he was alone, Maribel went next, followed by Jacob. Before Jacob could jump, Tamoren caught his arm.

"Tell them," he said solemnly. "They deserve to know."

Jacob didn't reply but he nodded gravely and Tamoren released him.

❄ ❄ ❄

The goblin wings were best described as a combination of a hand glider and a parachute. They fastened tightly onto the wearer's back and wrists, and, when on the ground, looked like an oversized cloak. When the wearer jumped, the cloth caught the rush of wind and billowed out, sending the wearer into a slow, steady descent, provided that she or he kept their arms out wide.

Once they had all reached the ground safely and discarded the goblin wings into a nearby stream, they moved away from the goblin city as fast as they could. Ben snuck one look back before they'd gotten too far away and thought he could see his father still watching them from high atop his palace tower.

It was early evening on the 23rd of December and the snow that had begun earlier in the day had refused to let up. Ben, being the shortest of the three and still nursing the injuries inflicted at his brother's hand, had the most trouble fighting his way through the thick coat of snow but his companions were patient and kept watch.

They alternated between walking and running all night long and into the early hours of the morning. Tamoren had given each of them a pack full of supplies before they had left and they ate sparingly from it as they moved. The combination of the food and the constant movement allowed them to stay, if not warm, at least not freezing.

When they felt they were a good enough distance away, they decided to take a break and try to get a few hours of sleep before making the final push. Jacob tried to convince them that it would be a good idea to find a town and try to get a ride back to Saint Louis but both Maribel and Ben knew that no one was likely to help a goblin that they met so close to the goblin city, regardless of the human company that he kept.

With that decided, they stopped under a bridge and built a fire in one of the drier spots where the snow accumulation wasn't as much. Maribel slept first. She protested that she was fine but was unconscious no sooner than she had laid her head down on her pack.

Jacob and Ben stared at the crackling fire. It was the first time they had been alone together since that morning in the lighthouse months before. There was a question burning in the back of Ben's mind that he had been too preoccupied before to bother asking but now seemed like the time.

"Why are you here?" he asked gently.

Jacob looked up at him. There was a sadness in his eyes that Ben had never seen before. These were definitely not the same eyes that had glared at him with such prejudiced anger only months before.

"I need to tell you something," he said.

"Sure," Ben replied.

"I'm the reason we're here," he said bluntly and without hesitation.

Ben frowned and shook his head. "I don't understand."

Jacob wrapped his arms around himself a little tighter as a gust of wind blew through their small, makeshift campsite.

"I sent a letter to Jotunfell a few months ago telling them that you were in Saint Louis. I didn't realize the full repercussions of your absence, but I guessed that they wouldn't have known where you were. Your brother got in contact with me last week and we came to an agreement that he would take you and only you. I'm here because Maribel came after you, and I knew it would be my fault if something happened to her."

Ben looked at the ground. He had known

Jacob disliked him but he would never have guessed this much.

"Why?" was all he could manage to say.

Jacob fell silent and for several tense moments, all that could be heard was the sound of the whistling wind, the crackling fire, and the soft breathing of Maribel.

"I never intended to be a lamplighter," Jacob said. "I was supposed to be a farmer, like my father before me, and his father before him. We had a small farm northeast of the city where I lived with my parents and my twin siblings, a boy and girl. We were happy.

"I was to turn fifteen in one week, the night that they came. A group of goblins, out of nowhere, turned up on our doorstep. They demanded food and shelter. Out of fear, my father gave them some bread and raw vegetables but said that we didn't have room to keep them all. Without a word, one of them drew his sword and cut him down. My mother told me to run and then she went after the twins who were asleep in our room. I was near the back door, so I got up and ran. I ran and I ran and I ran until my legs felt like they had caught fire and I couldn't breathe anymore. I stopped then, turned around, and went back. I knew what I would find by the bright orange glow on the horizon, but I went anyway.

"By the time I reached the farm, the goblins were gone. The house, the barn, even the fields were on fire. My father, mother, brother, and sister were all hanging limply from the tree in the front yard where I used to swing when I was a boy. My parents were each hanging from the ropes of that swing."

Jacob stopped speaking and once again, tense silence filled the air. This time, however, Ben was looking directly at the man who sat across the fire from him, and he had no idea what to say.

"I've hated goblins every second of every

minute of every day since then. I know that you're not like the others. I've always known that. But every time I look at you, I see the faces of the goblins in the doorway that stole my life from me."

Jacob broke off abruptly and turned away, but not before Ben noticed the unshed tears in his eyes.

"So, what happens now?" asked Ben, his throat unusually dry.

"Your father spared my life," said Jacob, fighting to regain his composure, "and I owe you recompense for my actions against you."

"You don't owe me anything," Ben said.

Jacob shook his head. "I do, and I'll think of a way to repay it. I don't think we can be friends as you and Maribel are, but I will try to be kind to you as best as I can."

Ben nodded, satisfied. In fact, given what had happened to Jacob, he felt as if *he* owed something to him but decided to let it go for now.

Maribel woke a half hour later and neither of them mentioned their conversation again the rest of the return journey.

14.

COMING HOME

It took all day and into the night before they saw the lights of the city in the distance. Jacob planned to speak to the guild master and accept full responsibility for their absence. He said it so firmly that neither Maribel nor Ben argued.

Finally, as a clock tower in the distance chimed three, Ben climbed into his own bed in the lighthouse and slept. It was one of those periods of sleep that you don't remember. You may recall lying down, getting comfortable, and then closing your eyes at the very least. Ben remembered nothing and dreamed of nothing. When he awoke, it felt as though it had only been a moment since he lay down but it was now after noon, and the sun was high in the sky.

As he sat up in bed and looked around at the small room, a quote from *A Christmas Carol* came to the forefront of his mind:

> "Yes! And the bedpost was his own. The bed was his own, the room was his own. Best and happiest of all, the time before him was his own . . ."

He reached under his bed and felt around for a few moments until his hand landed on a small stack of books tied together with a worn red ribbon. He untied the ribbon, laid the books out on his bed, and read the titles. *Little Women*, *Emma*, *Cricket on the Hearth*, *Sir Gawain and the Green Knight*, and *A Christmas Carol*. Each book had the same red ribbons placed at certain points in the stories, each describing a Christmas that he had never known.

As usual, he began and ended with *Little Women*, reading of two very different and yet similarly heartwarming holidays spaced one year apart. When he finished reading of that last Christmas, the sun was nearly set and his night watch would soon begin.

Ben crawled out of bed and got dressed. If he'd had a mirror, he would have been horrified at the face that looked back at him. He was still heavily bruised from the beating that his brother had given him. The cold had masked most of his pain but now that he was thoroughly thawed out, he felt it in full. It consumed every muscle in his body, and it took great effort to climb the stairs to the top of the lighthouse.

His watch had just started when he heard footsteps behind him. He turned slowly to see Maribel walking toward him.

"Happy Christmas!" she said, holding out a package to him. It seemed as though it had been a lifetime ago when he had first been dreaming about what Christmas might be like this year. So much had changed since then.

"Thanks," he said, his fingers trembling as he took the package. Though nervous and excited to receive his first Christmas gift, he couldn't help feeling guilty that he hadn't bought anything for her. It seemed as though she had read his thoughts, too, because she quickly said, "Don't worry, I don't need anything in return. It's your first Christmas."

Ben opened the package to reveal a hat and scarf. The hat was what he had heard people call a flat cap and it was gray and soft and he guessed that it was made of wool. The scarf was soft and thick, with alternating blue and gray stripes.

"You always look so cold," she said. "I thought you could use a nice hat and scarf."

Ben smiled and put the hat on, wincing at the pain in his arms as he did so. Noticing his discomfort, Maribel took the scarf and wrapped it around his neck.

"Thank you, truly. I love them!" And he meant it, knowing the words failed to express the full appreciation and emotion that he felt in that moment, but unsure how else to convey what was in his heart.

Maribel smiled back. "So, how are you enjoying your first Christmas?" she asked.

Ben thought back to the last few days, and how happy he was to be at the lighthouse again. He thought of his friendship with Maribel and his understanding with Jacob, and how, finally, he both knew his father and felt, if only a little bit, accepted. "Well, it's not exactly Dickens, but it's the best I've ever had."

They leaned on the railing and stared out across the river. Ben wondered what his father was doing at that moment. He had sacrificed his own happiness because he thought he had no other option. One day, Ben promised himself, he would free his father from that life and maybe bring him here.

Ben looked out at the lights of Saint Louis as evening descended. Snow had begun to fall from the sky once more and a single word stuck out in Ben's mind.

Home.

For the first time, he realized, he was indeed home. It was true that most of the city either despised him or feared him or both, but it was still about the best home that a good goblin could hope for.

AUTHOR'S NOTE

This book has been a little over four years in the making but this story is about eight times as old.

Ever since I was a child, I loved creating stories. Either by writing them, drawing them, or simply acting them out with my toys, I was constantly creating stories.

At an elementary school book fair, I picked up Bruce Coville's *Goblins in the Castle*, which changed my life, though I didn't really know it then. My ten-year-old mind was equally enraptured and terrified of the book, and the end result was a lifetime fascination with goblins.

Fast forward to about five years ago, when I first began reading R.A. Salvatore's Drizzt Do'Urden stories. One of his short stories, *Dark*

Mirror, concerns a goblin who is different from his peers. This goblin has a much darker outlook on life than my Ben does and his story definitely does not end happy, but I loved the idea of portraying goblins as something more than mindless bottom dweller villains and I wanted to see the idea expanded upon. So, I decided to write it myself and this book is the result (at least the first part of the result).

I'd like to thank my wife, Ashleigh, and my friend, Andrea Stolzer, for being my first readers and giving me confidence that this story might have a future. I'd like to thank my editor, Parisa Zolfaghari, for her enthusiasm and for turning my story into a book. I'd like to thank my family and friends for humoring me during the last decade every time I talked about my dream of becoming a published author. And last but not least, I'd like to thank my daughter, Viola, for just being the sweet, smart, funny girl that you are.

About the Author

David McElroy is a writer and designer who has been creating stories in one way or another since childhood. A chance pickup at an elementary school book fair began his fascination with goblins, and he's always believed they could be more than simple fodder for stalwart adventurers.

He lives in Lebanon, IL with his wife and daughter. The Good Goblin is his first published work.

Made in the USA
Middletown, DE
01 November 2017